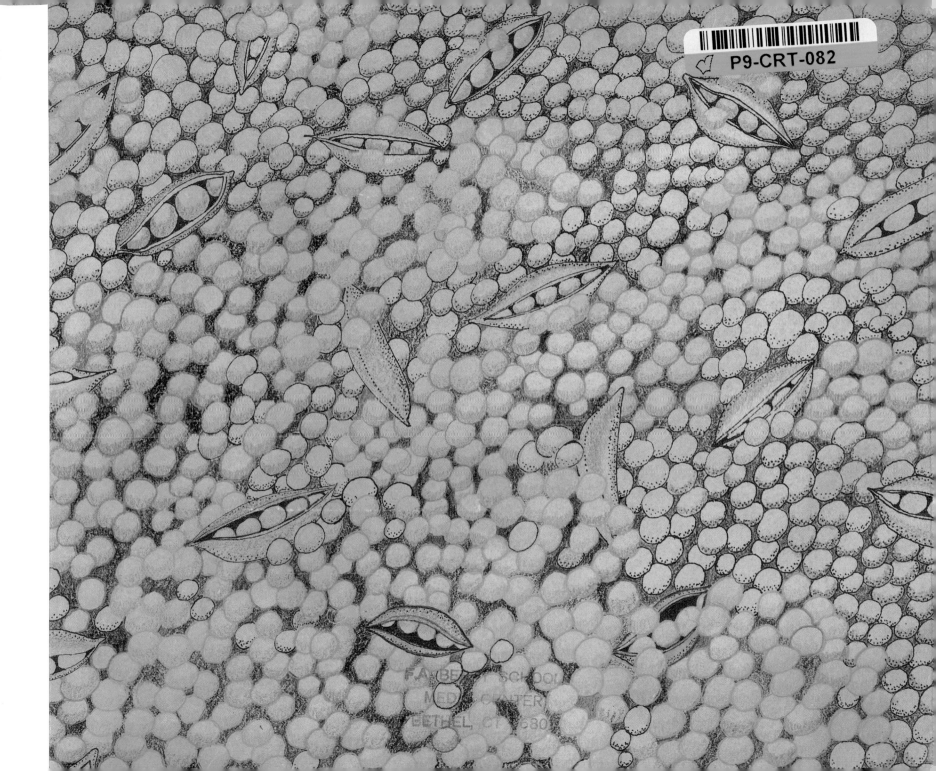

JUDITH CASELEY

Mr. Green Peas

Greenwillow Books, New York

Special thanks to Jack Neubert and his iguana

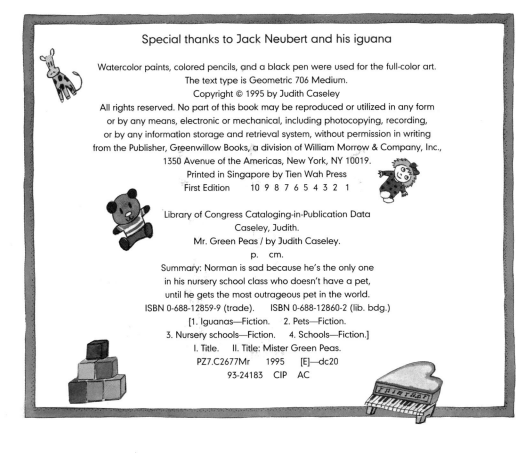

Watercolor paints, colored pencils, and a black pen were used for the full-color art.
The text type is Geometric 706 Medium.
Copyright © 1995 by Judith Caseley
All rights reserved. No part of this book may be reproduced or utilized in any form
or by any means, electronic or mechanical, including photocopying, recording,
or by any information storage and retrieval system, without permission in writing
from the Publisher, Greenwillow Books, a division of William Morrow & Company, Inc.,
1350 Avenue of the Americas, New York, NY 10019.
Printed in Singapore by Tien Wah Press
First Edition   10 9 8 7 6 5 4 3 2 1

Library of Congress Cataloging-in-Publication Data
Caseley, Judith.
Mr. Green Peas / by Judith Caseley.
p.   cm.
Summary: Norman is sad because he's the only one
in his nursery school class who doesn't have a pet,
until he gets the most outrageous pet in the world.
ISBN 0-688-12859-9 (trade).   ISBN 0-688-12860-2 (lib. bdg.)
[1. Iguanas—Fiction.   2. Pets—Fiction.
3. Nursery schools—Fiction.   4. Schools—Fiction.]
I. Title.   II. Title: Mister Green Peas.
PZ7.C2677Mr   1995   [E]—dc20
93-24183   CIP   AC

To Jenna and Mickey,
my own sweet peas

Norman Slope liked going to nursery school.

He liked wearing his brand-new backpack.

He liked having a cubbyhole with his name on it.

He liked crackers and juice at snacktime, even though cookies and milk at home with his mother tasted better.

When Toni, Norman's teacher, traced his outline on a big piece of paper, he liked coloring in his own brown eyes, his nose, his smile, and his favorite red shirt.

He enjoyed making a box out of Popsicle sticks that he could keep his treasures in, even if he didn't get to eat the Popsicles first.

He liked everything about nursery school, until Toni called them to the table and introduced them to the classroom pet, Herman the hamster.

Herman the hamster he loved.

When Toni asked if any of the children had pets, Arnie and Daniel and Erika had dogs, and Jenna and Stephanie had cats, and Jason had two parakeets, and Melissa had a turtle, and Sami had a gerbil.

Norman didn't have a pet. So he drew a picture of a cat with floppy ears like a dog and a green turtle shell on its back, a long black tail, and wings.

When Norman showed the picture to his parents, his mother said, "How... interesting. What is it?"

"It's my pet," said Norman. "It's the most outrageous pet in the world. Better than a plain old cat or a dog or a hamster or a parakeet. But one of those would do."

"I'm sorry, Norman," said his father. "I'm allergic to cat and dog hair."

"And hamsters and gerbils remind me of rats," said his mother.

"And a parakeet's chirping would drive us crazy," said his father.

Norman Slope moped for days. He put his picture of the most outrageous pet in the world on the wall in his bedroom. He left stuffed animals on his father's chair at breakfast time and a little pink mouse by his mother's coffee cup.

"We get the point, dear," said Mrs. Slope. "But no pets. The subject is closed."

But it wasn't. Because one day his father came home
smiling.

"I have a surprise for you," he said to Norman. "It's a part-
time pet. We'll take care of it for one month out of every
year, when my boss goes on vacation."

"A month I can handle," said Mrs. Slope.

"What is it?" said Norman.

"You'll never guess in a million years," said Mr. Slope,
and he left the house and returned with a covered cage.
Mr. Slope pulled the cover off the cage slowly.

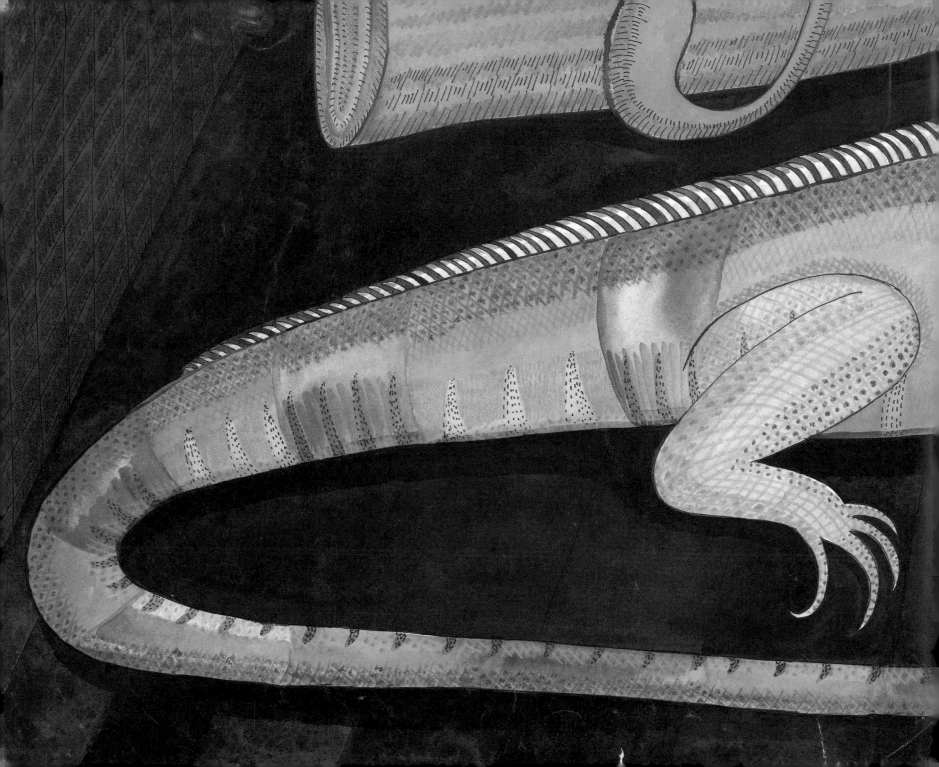

"It's a monster!" screamed Norman's mother.

"It's outrageous!" said Norman. "It's the most outrageous pet in the world!"

"It's an iguana," said Mr. Slope. "And I'm not allergic to him, and he won't chirp, and it's only for a month."

"He's better than a dog or a cat or a hamster or a gerbil," said Norman. "Does he bite?"

"He's a vegetarian, and very gentle," said Mr. Slope. "He's partial to peas."

"He's so . . . green," said Norman's mother. "But peas I can handle."

"We can call him Mr. Green Peas!" shouted Norman.

Norman drew a picture of Mr. Green Peas and brought
it to school the very next day to show Toni and the children.

"You saw it in the zoo?" said Toni.

"He lives at my house," said Norman.

"Norman is making it up," said Sami.

"He's cuckoo," said Arnie.

"No, I'm not," said Norman. But he could see that no one
believed him. And he thought of a plan.

He went home and told his mother what to write on a piece of paper, and his father made copies of it, and Norman gave them to Toni.

"It's a class trip to my house," explained Norman. "These are my permission slips."

Toni thought it was a great idea, and she passed the slips out to the children to be signed at home.

On the morning of the class trip Norman stayed home. He told Mr. Green Peas his breakfast would be late.

The doorbell rang. Norman let the children in. They looked as though they were about to see a scary movie. They filed in slowly.

"Here he is," said Norman, pointing to Mr. Green Peas, who was sitting on the sofa.

"This is his favorite spot," said Norman, while the children ooohed and ahhed. "You can give him breakfast if you want, Arnie."

Mr. Green Peas ate Arnie's big bowl of peas while Mrs. Slope gave the children cups of juice and mini muffins.

After breakfast Mr. Green Peas took a walk across the carpet, over to the window, and straight up the curtains.

"Outrageous!" said Arnie.

"I told you," said Norman.

Then Norman's mother passed out crayons and pieces of paper, and the children drew pictures of Mr. Green Peas. The children said good-bye and took their pictures of Mr. Green Peas home to their parents.

But Norman knew that no one would believe them.

Norman didn't care, because he had a plan.

Next year he would have a special class trip and let the children bring their parents when they came to visit the most outrageous pet in the world.

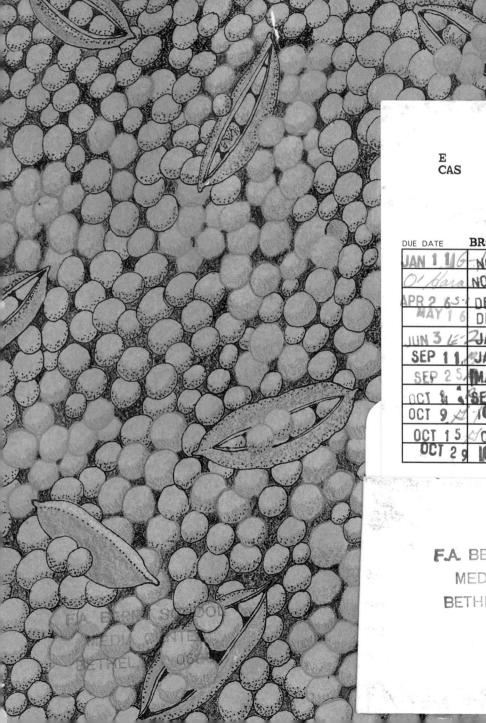

E
CAS

1S